When You Visit Grandma & Grandpa

by **Anne Bowen**

pictures by **Tomek Bogacki**

Carolrhoda Books, Inc. / Minneapolis

When you visit Grandma and Grandpa,
I tell my new baby brother,
you wake up early.
So early, it's still night outside,
and the moon's light
shines across your bed.

In the backseat
of the car
you snuggle,
sleepy and shivery,
under cozy blankets.

When you visit Grandma and Grandpa,
it helps to take lots of books,
three games, and all your crayons,
because their house is very far away.

Before Daddy even
drives three blocks,
you can't help asking,
"How much longer
'til we get there?"
And Mama will say,
"Not for awhile."

The car ride is long,
but when you get to
Grandma and Grandpa's
you will have
the best time ever!

In the spring,
I tell my new baby brother,
when rain
plink-plinks
on the porch roof
all day long,
Grandpa will perform
magic tricks,
singing, "Ala-ka-za-zoo,"
as he makes
a penny disappear
inside a blue hankie,
and pulls yellow daisies
from an old black hat.

And when the rain stops,
you'll get to splash-dance
through the puddles with Grandma
until you're soaking wet—
and you won't even get in trouble!

When you visit Grandma and Grandpa,
you sing all your favorite songs
along the way, especially,
"Miss Mary Mack, Mack, Mack,
all dressed in black, black, black . . ."
until Daddy says, "Enough!"

And then,
it's always good
to read a book for awhile.

In the summer, I tell my new baby brother,
you'll get to play hide-and-seek
with Grandma until way past dark.

Then you'll sit with Grandpa on the porch
watching fireflies flicker-dance
along the rose hedge,
their tiny moons of light
bobbing in the summer night.

When you visit Grandma and Grandpa,
you press your nose
against the car window,
listening to the zip-zip of cars
going by in blurry colors,
so fast you almost feel dizzy!

In the fall, I tell my new baby brother,
you can jump from Grandpa's porch
into the sweet crunch of leaves
piled high all over the yard.

You'll get to pick the biggest pumpkin
from the garden and watch Grandma
carve a jack-o'-lantern so scary
even Grandpa screams when he sees it!

When you visit Grandma and Grandpa,
you ask,
"Are we there yet?"
"Are we there yet?"
"Are we there yet?"
two times, five times, a HUNDRED times,
until Mama says, "Enough!"
and you say, "But how long?"
and Mama says, "Soon now. Very soon."

In the winter, I tell my new baby brother,
you will see new snow
zigzagging along
the porch railing like
Grandma's buttercream frosting.

And Grandpa
will help you make
the biggest snow fort ever,
bigger than the one
you made the year before.

When you visit Grandma and Grandpa,
you will bounce up and down
in the backseat of the car
as Daddy starts to slow down,
drives past a yellow house,
a mailbox painted sky blue,
three maple trees in a row.

Your heart will beat faster
as you lean forward,
looking and looking . . .

and then you will see lights
shining through their window,
and coming down
the stone steps of the porch—
GRANDMA! GRANDPA!

You will race out of the car
into their arms, hugging them
for a very long time.

And you will know,
I tell my new baby brother,
that ANYTIME
is the BEST TIME
to visit our Grandma and Grandpa.

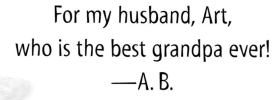

For my husband, Art,
who is the best grandpa ever!
—A. B.

For Mom and Dad, the best Parents,
Grandparents, and Great Grandparents.
—T. B.

Text copyright © 2004 by Anne Bowen
Illustrations copyright © 2004 by Tomek Bogacki

Carolrhoda Books, Inc.
A division of Lerner Publishing Group
241 First Avenue North
Minneapolis, MN 55401 U.S.A.

Website address: www.carolrhodabooks.com

Library of Congress Cataloging-in-Publication Data

Bowen, Anne, 1952-
When you visit Grandma and Grandpa / by Anne Bowen ; illustrations by Tomek Bogacki.
p. cm.
Summary: A sister explains to her new baby brother the excitement and activities surrounding a trip to Grandma and Grandpa's house.
ISBN: 1-57505-610-0 (lib. bdg. : alk. paper)
[1. Grandparents—Fiction. 2. Babies—Fiction. 3. Brothers and sisters—Fiction.] I. Bogacki, Tomasz, ill. II. Title.
PZ7.B671945Wh 2004
[E]—dc22
2003018050

Manufactured in the United States of America
1 2 3 4 5 6 – JR – 09 08 07 06 05 04